SPAGHETTI PARK

DyAnne DiSalvo

HOLIDAY HOUSE / New York

**For my father, who still denies he ever said,
"Spaghetti is the steak of life!"
(But I know better.)**

Special thanks to Jane Feder, Jean Marzollo, Mary Cash, Kathy Moore,
and the neighbors of Corona Heights, Queens, NY,
whose William F. Moore Park helped inspire this story

Text and illustrations copyright © 2002 by DyAnne DiSalvo
All Rights Reserved
Printed in the United States of America
The text typeface is Italian Old Style.
This artwork was created with gouache.
www.holidayhouse.com
First Edition

Library of Congress Cataloging-in-Publication Data

DiSalvo, DyAnne.
Spaghetti park / DyAnne DiSalvo.—1st ed.
p.   cm.
Summary: Angelo and his grandfather help rejuvenate a local park.
ISBN 0-8234-1682-8 (hardcover)
[1. Grandfathers—Fiction. 2. Parks—Fiction. 3. City and town life—Fiction.]

PZ7.D6224 Sp 2002
[E]—dc21   2001040605

Little by little our park became a place for neighborhood troublemakers to hang out. Zoomy, Jag, and Vinny played their boom box so loud that the old-timers gave up their benches. Richie and Grady whipped up the swings, so mothers quit bringing their children. Now nobody goes to the park anymore. Nobody, that is, except Grandpa and me.

These days, Grandpa is teaching me bocce. Bocce is like an Italian bowling game—and I am getting good. The long patch of dirt near the park's stone wall isn't a real bocce court, but it's all right for learning.

"Anybody can do that," Zoomy yells when I toss my underhand pitch.

"It's not so easy," I tell him back. "You don't even know how to play."

When my ball rolls crazy off the dirt, Richie runs to grab it.

"I know how to play this game," he says. "My grandpa taught me too."

My grandpa says that Richie's grandpa had a special way to toss the ball.

"He never told anyone his secret," says Grandpa. "Not even me."

Sometimes the old-timers come to watch while we practice during the day.

"Franco, franco," Mr. Cravelli shouts out. "Let the games begin."

"First I'll throw the little pallino," Grandpa says. The target ball zips across the dirt and stops before it gets to the end.

"Troppo piano! You threw it too easy," I tell him.

"Troppo forte! You threw it too hard," Richie shouts.

"Never mind," Mr. Rizzo warns him.

Green ball, red ball, green ball, and red ball. It's only a guess to say which toss will end up closest to the pallino.

The old-timers get to bragging about who *used* to play the best.

"I was the bocce champ so many times, people stopped counting," says Mr. Rizzo.

"I was so good, they made a statue of me," Mr. Donato tells him.

Each one likes to stretch the truth a little more than the other.

"Spaghetti benders!" Grady squeals. "Everyone knows that Richie's grandpa was the champ."

After Grandpa and I get our lemon ices, Richie hollers from across the street, "See you tomorrow. We'll be here."

"I'm telling my father," I say to Grandpa. "Those hangouts hog up the park."

My father belongs to the neighborhood group. Once a month they get together to discuss the local issues. Last month the group got the city to put up a traffic light on a busy corner. This month I'm going to the meeting too. And I can't wait to get there.

At the school, Officer Greg greets people at the door, while Grandpa and I set up chairs. Assembly Member Lopez sits up front. After everyone is settled in, my father reads from his pad.

"Mr. Gale says Clara Street has a lot of litter these days," he says.

"Why should we bother picking up litter today when there'll only be more tomorrow?" Mrs. Morgenstern wants to know.

"Things get done when people speak up," my father tells her. "That's why we're here."

"I think we should have a bocce ball court in the park across the street." Everyone turns to look at me.

"That's a good idea that Angelo has," Mr. Donato says.

Grandpa smiles and gives me a nudge.

"Wake up and smell the coffee!" Mrs. Morgenstern heckles. "Those hoodlums will never leave."

"She's right," Mr. Rizzo backs her up.

The whole downstairs is getting heated.

Assembly Member Lopez says, "If we all work together, we can make that park into something for everyone."

We agree to form a painting group to paint over the graffiti. Officer Greg recommends a gardening bunch for planting. Already the old-timers are spaghetti bending.

"My tomatoes will grow to be twice as big as grapefruits," Mr. Donato says.

"People will say my peppers taste the sweetest in the world," Mr. Cravelli tells him.

Every day we pick up trash and let ourselves be known. Still, most of the hangouts are up to their mischief. Whenever we sweep a pathway or plant a row of seedlings, the next day they are ruined.

"Enough is enough!" Mr. Rizzo says.

But I keep his mind on the new bocce court, and that always gets him working.

In one month's time, Assembly Member Lopez has petitioned enough funds from local businesses to begin construction on the court. The space is measured to lay down the planks and fill the first layer with sand. One time Richie helps rake the leaves.

"Big deal," Richie says when Jag and Vinny start to make fun of him.

Now every week gets a little bit closer to a grand-opening celebration. The new bocce court is not ready yet, but Grandpa and I try it out.

I learn the Great Grandpa Toss and the Grand Grandpa Roll. I also learn some tough kids are nicer when the whole gang isn't around.

"You're getting so good," Grady says, "they might name a street after you."

Grandpa smiles and whispers to me, "Now that's a spaghetti bender."

The next morning when Grandpa and I get to the park, we can't believe our eyes. All the benches that we had painted are covered with graffiti. The new swings are twisted, the checkerboard tables are muddy, and the little garden is crushed.

"And look what they did to the bocce ball court," I cry to Grandpa. Garbage cans are upside down with trash tossed everywhere.

By now everybody else has shown up.

"I knew this would happen," Mrs. Morgenstern says.

"That's it," Mr. Rizzo yells. "I'm finished."

And everyone else agrees.

My father scrambles to put together an emergency neighborhood meeting.

"We can't give up!" my father says. "The more we try, the better it gets."

"The more we try, the worse it gets," Mr. Cravelli hollers.

The place is in an uproar. I spot Grady and Richie sneak in the back.

"What are you doing here?" I say to Richie. "Do you want to wreck this place too?"

But Richie acts as if he's paying attention to the meeting.

Groups of neighbors are leaving in a huff till only a few of us are left.

"Anyone who wants this project to work should be there first thing tomorrow," my father calls after them.

"I'm not quitting," I tell Grandpa.

"I'm sticking with you," he tells me.

On the way home, the tough kids are out in front of the park as usual.
"There go the bocce players," somebody hollers.
But then I hear Richie say something to Zoomy and go nose to nose with him.

The next morning, I begin to worry. What if nobody else shows up to help?
My father puts one arm around me and the other one around Grandpa.

"I'm glad you two are part of the team," my father tells us both.

That's when I realize I like this team. It's the team I want to be on.

When we get to the park, Mr. Rizzo is waiting.

"Look at this," Mr. Rizzo says as he stretches out his hands.

Except for the graffiti and some of the planting, the whole park has been cleaned.
Richie stands in the middle of some tough kids who are holding rakes and
brooms.

"If bocce was good enough for my grandpa, then it's good enough for me,"
says Richie.

"It's our park too, you know," says Grady as he opens a can of paint for
Mr. Donato.

Mrs. Morgenstern gasps.

"There's always a few good apples in the bunch," Grandpa says to her.

"Do you think you can teach me that underhand pitch?" Zoomy asks me.

I fold my arms and squint my eyes. "It's not so easy," I tell him.

Well, our hardscrabble park turned out to be a place for everyone. Vinny, Jag, and some of the gang patrolled the square like Officer Greg and became part of the neighborhood watch group. Once in a while there were still bits of mischief but not like there used to be. The swings stayed busy, and the old-timers were back spaghetti bending on their benches.

On the grand-opening weekend, the neighborhood group staged a main event with music and food and dancing. All the helpers received certificates.

After the ribbon-cutting ceremony, my father gave me the little pallino. I stood with the target ball in my hands and looked down the new bocce court. Then I smiled at Grandpa as I turned to Richie and handed the ball to him.

Well, nobody ever spaghetti bends when they talk about what happened that day. They all say that it marked a new game, a new bowl. Because when Richie tossed the little pallino, it rolled in a way that was secretly familiar, and the old-timers cheered when they saw it.

"Franco, franco," I said so loud you could hear me a block away. "Let the games begin!"

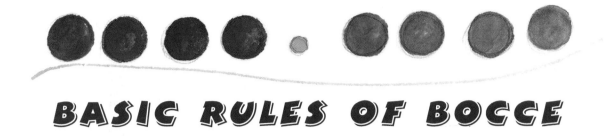

BASIC RULES OF BOCCE

The bocce court, or *campo,* should be reasonably smooth and flat. A grassy backyard or a gravel driveway is perfect! An official bocce court is about 75 feet long and about 12 feet wide.

The game is played with eight large bowling balls called *bocce balls* and one small target ball called a *pallino.* Half the *bocce balls* are a different color.

There are two teams. Each plays with a different color. The game can be played with one, two, or four players on each team.

The object of the game is for each team to try and roll its balls as close to the *pallino* as possible.

Teams toss a coin to see who goes first. The starting team gets to pick the color of ball it wants to use.

The first player rolls the *pallino* within the court or playing area. The opposing team rolls its *bocce ball* as close to the *pallino* as possible.

If the opposing team gets its ball close to the *pallino,* the starting team rolls its *bocce ball* and tries to knock the opposing team's ball away.

When all the balls have been played, the points are counted. A team gets a point for every ball that is closer to the *pallino* than the closest opposing team's ball.

The first team to score sixteen points is the champ—and that's no spaghetti bender.

You can find out more about bocce from the organizations and websites below:

United States Bocce Federation
44 Park Lane
Park Ridge, Illinois 60068
847-692-6223
www.bocce.com

The Bocce Standards Association
www.boccestandardsassociation.org